# NEW PIECES FOR FLUTE: BOOK

## GRADES 5 & 6

© 1978 by The Associated Board of the Royal Schools of Music
14 Bedford Square, London WC1B 3JG

Printed in England
A.B.1639

# PAN PASTORAL

Grade 5

John Hall Op. 55 No. 4

# CIRCUS-PONY

Stephen Dodgson

# ARABESQUE

Joseph Horovitz

# SCHERZANDO

Richard Stoker

# DANCE

Christopher Brown

* 2nd time this last chord sub *f*

# PASTORALE

# PASTORALE

Grade 6

Timothy Baxter

# RONDINO

Grade 6

Timothy Baxter

# PERPETUUM MOBILE

Grade 6

John Lambert

To Henri Jayles
# Prélude Français

Bryan Kelly

The Associated Board's series of new
pieces for wind instruments covers Grades 3—6.
Two books are available for each instrument:
bassoon, clarinet, flute and oboe.

For further details of these pieces
and for a list of all the Board's publications,
please write to the Publishing Department,
14 Bedford Square, London WC1B 3JG.